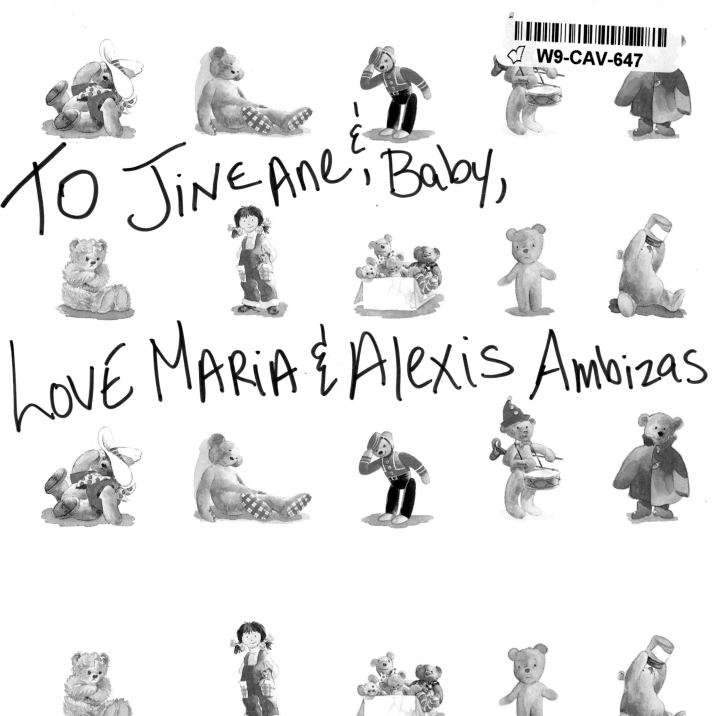

To Jineane & Baby,

Love Maria & Alexis Ambizas

TEDDY
TALES

For Peter
S. G.
For my father
P. U.

First published in the UK by Orchard Books, a division of the Watts Publishing Group,
96 Leonard Street, London.

This edition published by Barnes & Noble, Inc., by arrangement with Orchard Books

1997 Barnes & Noble Books

ISBN 0-7607-0357-4

Printed and bound in Spain

00 01 M 9 8 7 6 5 4 3 2

Gráficas

TEDDY
TALES

Sally Grindley

Illustrated by Peter Utton

BARNES
&NOBLE
BOOKS
NEW YORK

C·O·N·T

E · N · T · S

· HONEY · POT · BEAR ·

Honey Pot Bear had a great big honey pot, but that great big honey pot was empty.

"A honey pot with no honey is not a lot of good," she thought to herself.

So she decided to do something about it.

In the kitchen cupboard was a honey pot with lots of honey in it. Honey Pot Bear knew that because Samuel often had honey on toast for breakfast.

"I'll have some of that honey," she thought.

One night, when everyone in the house was asleep, she tiptoed downstairs with her honey pot and into the kitchen. She dragged a stool over to the cupboard, climbed up on it, and opened the cupboard door. There was the honey pot, full to the brim with honey.

7

"Yum!" said Honey Pot Bear, licking her lips at the thought of all that honey. "Yum, yum!" Honey Pot Bear put her empty pot down next to the full one. Then she picked up the full one and tried to open it.

"It's a bit stiff," she said, as the stool wobbled.

She stuck her paw in the pot and pulled it out again, all covered with sticky honey. She licked it, MMM! And again, YUM! And again, DELICIOUS! as it ran down her leg and onto the floor.

Then she lifted up the cupboard pot and tipped it over into her pot. Some of the honey ran into her pot. Some of it dripped onto the cupboard. Some of it dripped onto the stool. Some of it dripped onto the floor. When her pot was half full and the cupboard pot was half empty, Honey Pot Bear thought she had enough. She picked up her pot and started to climb down from the stool.

WHOA!

WHOA! the stool wobbled, and WHOOOAAAH! it wobbled again, and WHOOOOOAAAAAHHHHHH! Honey Pot Bear lost her balance and

CRASH! she and the stool fell to the floor.

The half-full honey pot landed upside down on Honey Pot Bear's tummy and runny honey trickled down her sides.

"Ugh!" she said. "Honey's not funny when it's running over your tummy."

One very sticky bear picked herself up and crept back upstairs, clutching her very sticky honey pot, and leaving a very sticky trail behind her.

No one, of course, could guess what had happened, because bears don't do that sort of thing, do they? Samuel thought it must have been Honey Pot Bear, but Mom still thinks it was Samuel . . .

· THE · RAGGEDY · BEARS ·

The Raggedy Bears were hospital bears. They lived in an old cardboard box in the children's ward. There were four of them: Charlie, Etta, Pammy, and Appleshaw.

The trouble with the Raggedy Bears was that they had been loved a bit too

much. Loved until the stitches had broken around Charlie's foot and the beans had fallen out; loved until the fur had worn away on Etta's tummy; loved until Pammy's ear was hanging by its last thread; and loved until Appleshaw's nose had been rubbed away.

But they didn't mind, not a bit. When another sick child picked one of them

14

up, tucked them under an arm, and wandered back to bed for a cuddle, the Raggedy Bears forgot their own sore spots.

Then one day a nurse picked them up, one by one, and shook her head sadly.

"These bears are really getting a bit old," she said. "Look, this poor soul's losing his beans, this one's got a bald tummy, this one's ear is coming off, and this one has lost his nose and has a hole in his neck."

"But we love them," came a little voice from one of the beds. "They're our friends."

That was just what the Raggedy Bears wanted to hear. They loved the children and they knew that their cuddles helped the children to get better.

"Couldn't they have an operation?" the little voice said. "Couldn't you mend their feet and their tummies and their ears and all their sore places?"

The Raggedy Bears waited quietly for the reply. They were scared of having an operation, but if it made them better, they could stay in the children's ward and carry on helping children through *their* operations.

"Well, all right," said the nurse. "I'm not promising anything, but we'll see what we can do."

For the next week the Raggedy Bears were stuffed and stitched and fluffed up and dressed until their sore spots had

disappeared. And when they looked in
the mirror and saw their new selves,
they danced with joy.

"Look at my red socks and yellow
bow tie!" said Charlie.

"Look at my furry tummy!" said
Etta.

"I can hear again properly!" said
Pammy.

"Look at my beautiful nose!" said
Appleshaw.

17

"We're not Raggedy Bears anymore. We're Better Bears!"

And they all laughed.

The Better Bears were taken back to the children's ward where the children cheered and cheered, HIP HIP HOORAY! And the Better Bears are still there now, waiting to cuddle more children, who will tuck them under their arms, and carry them to their beds to make themselves feel better.

· TOO · BIG · BEAR ·

Too Big Bear sat on the floor in the corner of Tom's bedroom.

He looked at all the toys having fun on Tom's chest of drawers. He looked and his tummy told him that he wasn't happy. He wasn't happy because he was too big.

Too big to go on the bed. Too big to ever be taken out by Tom. Too big to do anything but sit in the corner and watch everyone else having fun.

Too big to be loved.

Every day Too Big Bear had the same unhappy thoughts. Sometimes Tom and his friends would pull him out of his corner and jump on him, but that didn't make him feel loved, just bruised.

Then along came Little Kitten Mog.

Too Big Bear heard a fast and squeaky PRRR PRRR PRRR PRRR. Too Big Bear felt whiskers and a wet nose tickling the pads of his feet, PRRR PRRR PRRR. Too Big Bear saw two bright eyes, two pointed ears, and a round, fluffy face purring over his knees, PRRR PRRR PRRR.

Two tiny paws stepped onto his leg.

Two more paws jumped up behind. Little Kitten Mog kneaded the bear's big, soft tummy, made herself comfy, and settled down to sleep.

And that's where she slept every day after that.

And Too Big Bear smiled every day after that, while his tummy and his head told him he was happy.

· POCKET · BEAR ·

Pocket Bear was tiny, small enough to fit into your pocket. That's where she lived most of the time—in Emily's pocket. She went everywhere with her.

"No bear's been to as many places as

I have," she would boast. "What a well-traveled bear I am."

Pocket Bear went to nursery school, she went shopping, she went to the swimming pool (though she wasn't allowed into the water), she went to the park, to the beach, and once she even went up in an airplane.

"We went right up into the clouds." she said. "Can you believe it? Bet you wish *you* could go out."

Every time Pocket Bear went out, she

would come back and say to the other toys:

"You'll never guess where I've been today, while you've all been stuck here doing nothing."

That, of course, made the other toys very angry.

"Stop boasting," said Snow Bear at last. "One day you'll find yourself somewhere that you really don't want to be."

And that's just what happened.

One day Emily was sitting in a chair watching television. Pocket Bear was in her pocket. Suddenly she toppled over the top of the pocket and onto the chair. Then, as Emily moved around, Pocket Bear fell down inside the chair.

"Help!" she shouted, but, of course, humans can't hear bears.

It was dark inside the chair, and very noisy. Every time Emily moved, it

AAAH!

scratched and squeaked. Pocket Bear stuck her paws in her ears and wondered what to do. When she took her paws away, she heard Emily turn the television off, and suddenly it went darker still. Emily had turned off the light and was going out of the room!

"Don't leave me!" shouted Pocket Bear. "I'm scared of the dark!"

But, of course, humans can't hear bears. Bears can hear other bears, but bears can't move around until after midnight.

Bendy Bear and Bow Tie Bear heard Pocket Bear's cries, but they couldn't do anything about them.

"No one will find her," they said to each other. "She'll just have to wait for us."

And they couldn't help thinking that perhaps she might learn a lesson.

So Pocket Bear sat all alone, a very, very frightened bear, and wondered whether anyone would ever find her again.

At the stroke of midnight, Bendy Bear and Bow Tie Bear climbed down from their shelf and ran to the chair.

"Are you all right, Pocket Bear?" they shouted.

A muffled, frightened voice replied, "Yes, but please get me out."

Bow Tie Bear climbed up the arm of the chair and undid his bow tie.

"Grab hold of this," he yelled.

And he pushed his bow tie down the side of the chair. Bendy Bear held onto Bow Tie Bear's feet and together they pulled and pulled and pulled until

POP!

out popped Pocket Bear, and they fell in
a heap on the floor.

"Oh, thank you, thank you," she

cried. "I was so frightened in there. I might never have been found."

After that, Pocket Bear never boasted again about where she had been and what she had done, and the other bears liked her a lot better.

· CURLY · BEAR ·

Curly Bear had curly fur, and he hated it.

"Why can't I have straight fur like other bears? Curly fur is for she-bears and I'm a he-bear."

The other bears told him not to be so silly, and that his curly fur suited him.

But Curly Bear wouldn't listen. He

tried combing his fur with water. That made it go straight, but as soon as it was dry, it went curly again.

He tried plastering it down with Timothy's mom's hair mousse. That made an awful mess everywhere, but it did make his fur go straight—and very, very stiff. Timothy's mom found him and put him in the washing machine. He didn't like that one bit. When she took him out and dried him, his fur went curly again.

So Curly Bear tried Timothy's dad's hair oil. That made his fur go very straight and gave it a beautiful shine. But it also made him so slippery that he kept falling off the shelf, and he didn't like that one bit. Timothy's mom found him and put him in the washing machine again. And when she dried him his fur went all curly again.

Curly Bear hated his curly fur so much that he hid himself in a cupboard. He was sure the other bears laughed at his curls. But he was wrong. Old Bear,

whose fur was worn away, and Tough Talk Ted, whose fur was cropped short, both wished they had fur like Curly Bear. And Bella the Ballerina Bear thought Curly Bear was the most handsome bear she had ever seen.

It was Bella who found Curly Bear hidden away in the cupboard.

"What are you hiding in here for?" she asked.

Curly Bear said that he didn't want to see anyone, that he hated his curly fur,

35

and that he knew everyone was laughing at him.

Bella threw her arms around him and gave him a great big hug and told him that he was the most handsome bear in the world and shouldn't be so silly.

Curly Bear didn't believe her at first. But, after a while, he saw that perhaps his curly fur wasn't so bad after all. And after a little while longer, he began to like his curly fur. And now, if you asked him, he wouldn't change it for the world.

· BELLBOY · BEAR ·

Bellboy Bear lived in the toy department of a great big store. He hoped that one day someone would buy him and take him home. He wasn't in any hurry, though, for this store had an

elevator, and he wanted to ride in it.

One night, when all the people had gone home and the lights had been turned out, Bellboy Bear climbed down from his shelf and ran to the elevator. He pressed the button on the wall. The elevator whirred into action. Bellboy Bear waited excitedly. DING DONG! The doors slowly opened and Bellboy Bear jumped in. Then he pressed the button with a number 1 on it.

"Mind the doors, please," he said, though there was no one to get in or out.

The doors closed and up, up, up he went to the first floor. When the elevator stopped, the doors opened, and Bellboy Bear jumped out. Then he jumped back in and pressed the button with a G on it.

"Mind the doors, please," he said again.

The doors closed and down, down, down he went to the ground floor.

"This is fun," thought Bellboy Bear.

Up and down he went, over and over again.

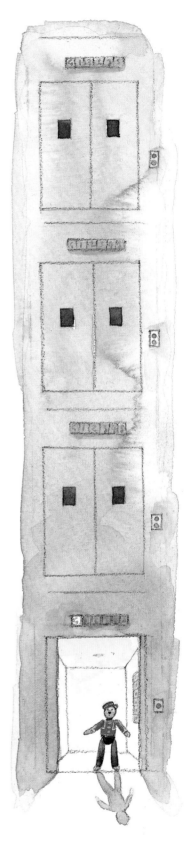

When he reached the ground floor for
the eleventh time, the doors opened, and
he had the shock of his life. There,
standing waiting for the elevator, were
all the other bears, stuffed toys, and
dolls from the toy department.

"We want to come, too!" they all said. And with that, they pushed and shoved and pushed and shoved until every last paw and frilly bow was squashed inside the elevator.

"Mind the doors, please," said Bellboy Bear loudly.

Up, up, up they went to the first floor.
When the doors opened they all jumped
out. But instead of getting back in
again, a hundred bears, stuffed toys,
and dolls ran around the store
with great whoops of delight.

"Look at this! Look at these! WOW! Just take a look at these!" they all shouted, as they discovered food and games and computers and a million things they had never seen before.

"Elevator Number One is about to depart," yelled Bellboy Bear, thoroughly enjoying his new job.

A hundred bears, stuffed toys, and dolls rushed back to the elevator and shoved and pushed their way in.

"Mind the doors, please," said Bellboy Bear. He pressed G and down, down, down they went again. When they reached the ground floor and the doors opened, no one moved.

"We want to go to the top floor," said a voice.

"We want to go to the top floor," shouted a hundred voices.

"I can't reach the top button," said Bellboy Bear, in dismay.

A big, strong-looking bear pushed his way forward and dashed into the store. Before Bellboy Bear could ask what he was doing, he came back with a stool and put it under the buttons.

"There you are, pal. Stand on that," he growled.

Bellboy Bear climbed up on the stool, pushed the button with a number 5 on it, and said: "Mind the doors, please." He felt his tummy go all funny as the elevator went up and up and up.

Once again, a hundred bears, stuffed toys, and dolls rushed out of the elevator and around the store, bouncing on beds,

climbing on chairs, and rolling each other
up in rugs.

"Elevator Number One about to depart,"
yelled Bellboy Bear. Down, down,
down they went, but suddenly the elevator
stopped with a CLUNK, and the doors
stayed shut. Bellboy Bear pressed G but
nothing happened.

"We're stuck," he said.

"We're stuck!" shouted a hundred
voices. "Let us out!" But nothing they
did would make the elevator move.

"We'll have to wait until someone finds us," said Bellboy Bear.

One by one, the toys sat down on the floor, snuggled up together, and went to sleep. That's where the store's manager found them the next morning. No one will ever know how a hundred bears, stuffed toys, and dolls from the toy department came to be fast asleep on the floor of Elevator Number One. No one, that is, except you and me.

· SAD · BEAR ·

Sad Bear never smiled. It didn't matter what he did or where he went or who he was with, he never, ever smiled. When Susie took him out with her, he didn't smile. When the other toys played games at night, he didn't smile. Even when someone tickled his tummy, he didn't smile. He just looked sad.

Sad Bear wanted to smile. Oh, how he wanted to smile! But he couldn't. Whoever had stitched his mouth at the toy factory had stitched a stiff, straight black line. Try as he might, Sad Bear couldn't make the corners turn up.

When no one else was looking, Sad Bear would sit in front of the mirror and stare at himself and try and try and try to make his smile work.

He told himself funny jokes, but he couldn't smile.

He tickled his chin with a feather, but he couldn't smile.

He made ugly faces at himself, but he couldn't smile.

The other toys thought he was a pain. And when he sat staring at himself in the mirror they thought he was vain.

Until one day Dungaree Bear saw tears running down his face and asked him what was the matter.

"I'm unhappy because I can't smile even when I'm very happy," said Sad Bear. "My mouth is stitched too tight."

When Dungaree Bear heard this, she gathered the other toys around her and told them Sad Bear's story.

"We must help him," she said.

That night, when Sad Bear was fast asleep, Dungaree Bear and Moon Bear tiptoed over to him with a needle and a spool of black thread. Very, very gently,

52

being careful not to wake him, they stitched two stitches at one end of his mouth and another two stitches at the other end of his mouth.

When Sad Bear woke up in the morning, he felt different. He thought he felt his mouth twitch. He thought he felt a smile coming when he saw the sun was shining. He rushed over to the mirror and saw that something about his face had changed.

"I look happy," he thought.

"I look happy," he said.

A big smile broke across his face.

"I *am* happy," he yelled.

And he was never sad again.

· RUM · TE · TUM · TED ·

Rum Te Tum Ted had a drum, RUM-
TE-TUM. When someone wound him
up, he r-r-rummed and he t-t-tummed
and he rat-a-tat-a-tatted, and he
hummed and he whirred and he
was as happy as can be.

Then along came Big Bass Bear. He was bigger and he was louder than Rum Te Tum Ted. And he had a drum that was twice as big as Rum Te Tum Ted's. When someone wound him up, he b-b-boomed and he b-b-banged and he walloped and he crashed. Then he laughed and he laughed at Rum Te Tum Ted.

"You're not as good as me," said Big Bass Bear. "I'm bigger and I'm louder, and, quite simply, I'm the best."

Rum Te Tum Ted felt sad. Now that Big Bass Bear was there, he was never allowed to drum on his own. When someone wound him up, they wound up Big Bass Bear as well.

"Give up," said Big Bass Bear. "No one can hear you. Bet you can't even hear yourself."

So Rum Te Tum Ted gave up. His arms went stiff, his legs went stiff, and the key in his back would no longer turn.

Sometime later, Tambourine Ted and Jingle Bells Bear appeared by his side. When someone wound them up, they tapped and they jingled and they ting-a-ling-linged. But they were never allowed to play unless Big Bass Bear played too.

Tap jingle ting-a-ling-ling BOOM BANG BOOM!

Rap jangle ring-a-ding-ding CRASH BANG WALLOP!

"Wow, this is great!" said Big Bass Bear one day, when the three had played together. "Why don't we form a band?"

Tambourine Ted and Jingle Bells Bear didn't answer. This Big Bass Bear was so loud that they didn't want to play with him if they could help it. They looked at Rum Te Tum Ted.

"What's wrong with him?" they asked.

"Oh, he's no good," said Big Bass Bear. "Doesn't know how to drum.

He gave up in the end."

"That's sad," said Tambourine Ted.

That night Tambourine Ted and Jingle Bells Bear looked at Rum Te Tum Ted again.

"Do you think we can get him to play?" said Tambourine Ted.

"Let's try," said Jingle Bells Bear. They went over to Rum Te Tum Ted.

"Don't know why you're bothering," said Big Bass Bear.

Rum Te Tum Ted had been listening, and as they touched his key, he shivered with excitement. The stiffness went from his arms and legs, and when the key turned in his back he lifted up his drumstick and—*rum-te-tum*!—he

Rat-a-tat-tat Rat-a-tat-tat Rum-te-tum Rum-te-tum

played his first drumbeat in months.

"Awful, isn't it?" said Big Bass Bear. "Wind me up and I'll show you how it's done."

Tambourine Ted looked at Jingle Bells Bear.

Jingle Bells Bear looked at Tambourine Ted.

Tambourine Ted wound up Jingle Bells Bear.

Jingle Bells Bear wound up Tambourine Ted.

And they played and played with Rum Te Tum Ted.

"Hey, what about me?" said Big Bass Bear.

"We don't need you," said the others. And that was the beginning of the Night Bears' Band!

· WELLIE · BEAR ·

Wellie Bear wore smart red wellington boots and a bright blue plastic raincoat. But Wellie Bear wasn't a happy bear.

"Hrrmp! I'm fed up with being indoors," he moaned to himself. "I am a Wellie Bear. I want to get wet. I want to jump in puddles. And I'm going to!"

The next day it began to pour with rain. When everyone had gone to bed and snores rumbled around the house, Wellie Bear tiptoed over to the window and climbed out onto the sill.

"It's raining, it's pouring,
They are all a'snoring,
And I'm going SPLASHING!"

WHEEE!

With that, he slid down the drainpipe
—WHEEE!—and landed with a bump
among the crocuses.

64

"I'm wet," he shouted. "I've got a wet bottom and wet paws. Now for wet boots!"

Wellie Bear stomped off down the path on a puddle hunt. The first puddle he came to was rather small, but that didn't matter to a bear who had never met a puddle before. He lifted one foot up and

SPLASH!

down it came into the puddle. He lifted the other foot and—SPLASH!—down that one came into the puddle too.

65

Left SPLASH, right SPLASH, left SPLASH, right SPLASH, left SPLASH, right SPLASH.

"My boots are wet, my boots are wet! That's what boots are for!" yelled Wellie Bear. "Now for a bigger puddle."

Ten steps further on was a puddle that made Wellie Bear's eyes water. He had never seen such a huge puddle.

"Wow," he shouted. "Count to three and in I go. 1—2—3—jump!"

And he jumped into the air and landed in the puddle with a—SPLASH!—that soaked him to the fur and filled his boots with water. He got out of the puddle and jumped in again— SPLASH!—and again—SPLASH! A soggier bear you have never seen.

Wellie Bear was now very cold. It was time to go home. He squished his way back to the house. But he couldn't climb up the drainpipe as easily as he had slid down it. It was far too slippery.

"What a silly bear I am," he shivered. "Soaking wet, freezing cold, and stuck outside."

He made his way around to the front of the house, crept under the doormat, and that's where he stayed until he was found in the morning.

"Maybe I'll try the bath next time," thought Wellie Bear, as he hung on the clothesline to dry, with his raincoat and boots hanging beside him.

· TEXAN · TED ·

Texan Ted couldn't sleep.

Christopher kept fidgeting. First he turned this way, and banged Texan Ted on the arm. OUCH!

Then he turned that way, and knocked Texan Ted on the ear.

Next he turned upside down, and kicked Texan Ted on the nose. That made Texan Ted sneeze. A-A-A-TCHOOO!

Then he rolled right over and pushed Texan Ted out of bed. AAAH! BUMP!

Texan Ted rubbed his head. He tried to climb back into the bed. He grabbed hold of the blanket and heaved. HEAVE! But his arms weren't strong enough.

He sat back on the floor and shivered. It was warm in Christopher's bed. It was cold on the floor.

Where was he going to sleep?

Texan Ted tried the bottom shelf of the bookcase, but that was too hard.

He tried the polka dot beanbag, but that was too soft.

Then he saw that the bottom drawer of the dresser was open. He climbed in between Christopher's sweaters, snuggled up tight, and that was just right.

Soon he was fast asleep.

Goodnight!